AMAZING FACES

To Charles John Egita
Forever amazing . . .
—L.B.H.

For my precious Crystal
—C.S.

Acknowledgments Thanks are due to the following for use of works in this collection: Joseph Bruchac for "Aunt Molly Sky." Copyright © 2010 by Joseph Bruchac. Used by permission of the author, who controls all rights. Mary E. Cronin for "Firefighter Face." Copyright © 2010 by Mary E. Cronin. Used by permission of the author, who controls all rights. Curtis Brown, Ltd. for "Amazing Face" by Rebecca Kai Dotlich. Copyright © 2010 by Rebecca Kai Dotlich; "Miss Stone" by Nikki Grimes. Copyright © 2002 by Nikki Grimes. Originally published by Creative Classroom Publishing LLC; "Hamburger Heaven" by Lee Bennett Hopkins. Copyright © 2010 by Lee Bennett Hopkins; "High in the Sky" by Pat Mora. Copyright © 2010 by Pat Mora; "Young Soldier" by Prince Redcloud. Copyright © 2010 by Prince Redcloud; "Karate Kid" by Jane Yolen. Copyright © 1996 by Jane Yolen. Originally published by Harcourt. All reprinted by permission of Curtis Brown, Ltd. HarperCollins Publishers for an excerpt from "Summer," in *My Chinatown* by Kam Mak. Copyright © 2002 by Kam Mak. Used by permission of HarperCollins Publishers. Lee Bennett Hopkins for "Hero" by Tom Robert Shields. Copyright © 2010 by Tom Robert Shields. Used by permission of Lee Bennett Hopkins for the author. J. Patrick Lewis for "Abuela." Copyright © 2010 by J. Patrick Lewis. Used by permission of the author, who controls all rights. Jude Mandell for "I'm the One." Copyright © 2010 by Jude Mandell. Used by permission of the author, who controls all rights. Jane Medina for "Me x 2/Yo x 2." Copyright © 2010 by Jane Medina. Used by permission of the author, who controls all rights. Random House, Inc. for "My People," from *The Collected Poems of Langston Hughes* by Langston Hughes, edited by Arnold Rampersad with David Roessel, Associate Editor, copyright © 1994 by The Estate of Langston Hughes. Used by permission of Alfred A. Knopf, a division of Random House, Inc. Carole Boston Weatherford for an excerpt from "Which Way to Dreamland?" Copyright © 2010 by Carole Boston Weatherford. Used by permission of the author, who controls all rights. Janet S. Wong for "Living Above Good Fortune." Copyright © 2010 by Janet S. Wong. Used by permission of the author, who controls all rights.

Collection copyright © 2010 by Lee Bennett Hopkins
Illustrations copyright © 2010 by Chris Soentpiet
All rights reserved. No part of this book may be reproduced, transmitted, or stored in an information retrieval system in any form or by any means, electronic, mechanical, photocopying, recording, or otherwise, without written permission from the publisher.
LEE & LOW BOOKS Inc., 95 Madison Avenue, New York, NY 10016
leeandlow.com
Manufactured in China by RR Donnelley Limited, August 2017
Book design by Christy Hale
Book production by The Kids at Our House
The text is set in Charlotte Sans Book
The illustrations are rendered in watercolor
(hc) 10 9 8 7 6 5 4
(pb) 10 9 8 7 6 5 4 3
First edition

Library of Congress Cataloging-in-Publication Data
Amazing faces / selected by Lee Bennett Hopkins ; pictures by Chris Soentpiet. — 1st ed.
p. cm.
Summary: "Poems focusing on universal emotions, as expressed by poets from diverse backgrounds, including Joseph Bruchac, Nikki Grimes, Lee Bennett Hopkins, Pat Mora, Janet S. Wong, and many others"—Provided by publisher.
ISBN 978-1-60060-334-1 (hardcover: alk. paper) ISBN 978-1-62014-223-3 (pb)
1. Emotions—Juvenile poetry. 2. Children's poetry, American. I. Hopkins, Lee Bennett. II. Soentpiet, Chris K., ill.
PS595.E56A43 2010   811.008'09353—dc22   2009022789

AMAZING FACES

POEMS SELECTED BY
LEE BENNETT HOPKINS

PICTURES BY
CHRIS SOENTPIET

LEE & LOW BOOKS INC.
NEW YORK

AMAZING FACE

Amazing, your face.
Amazing.

It shows there will be trails to follow,
porches to wave from, wonder from,
play on.

It shows you will sail ships,
paint stars,
carve pumpkins,
hours,
years.

You will climb stalks,
greet giants,
crawl before you walk.
And you will fly
And you will fall.
And you will fly again.

Amazing, your face.
It shows you will watch from a window,
whisper to a friend,
ride a carousel,
melt candy on your tongue.

Amazing, your face.
Amazing.

REBECCA KAI DOTLICH

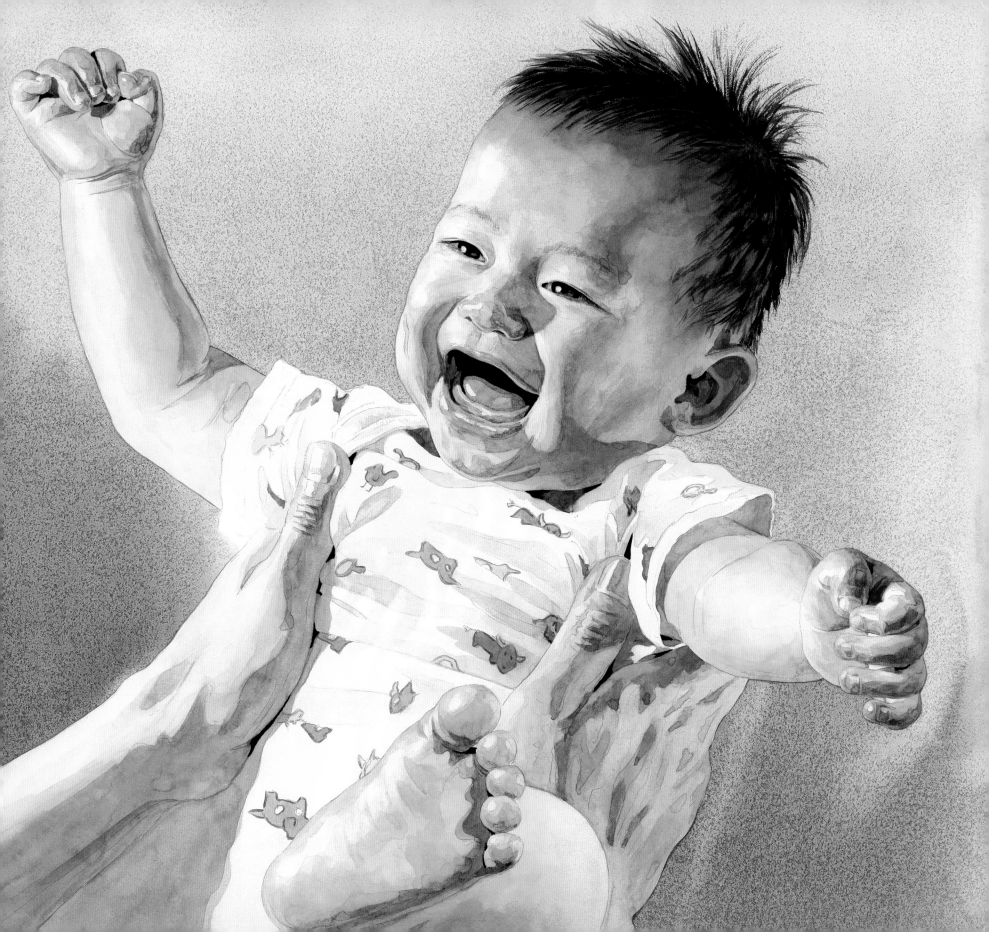

from

MY CHINATOWN

Twelve hours every day
the needle on her sewing machine
gobbles up fabric,
turning miles of cloth
into pants and jackets, skirts and dresses.
After supper I sit beside my mother,
listening to the hum of the motor,
the soft chatter
of the hungry needle.

Sometimes I fall asleep beside her,
the sound of her work
a lullaby.

KAM MAK

from

WHICH WAY TO DREAMLAND?

How in the world do dreams get
 in your head?
Do they hide with dust bunnies
 under the bed?

Do dreams spring from seeds
 sprouted deep in your mind,
creep while you sleep into vines
 you can climb?

How in the world do dreams get
 in your head?
Do they leap from the pages of books
 you have read?

Do dreams raise the bedsheets
 as if hoisting sails
to cruise behind dolphins and
 chase humpback whales?

Which way to Dreamland?
 Don't trouble your mind.
Close your eyes sleepyhead.
 Follow the signs.

CAROLE BOSTON WEATHERFORD

ME x 2

I read times two.
I write times two.
I think, I dream,
    I cry times two.

I laugh times two.
I'm right times two.
I sing, I ask,
    I try times two.

I do twice as much
    As most people do.
'Cause most speak one,
    But I speak two!

YO x 2

Leo por dos.
Escribo por dos.
Pienso y sueño
    Y lloro por dos.

Yo río por dos.
Grito por dos.
Canto, pregunto,
    Intento por dos.

Hago mucho más
    Que hacen todos ellos,
Porque yo hablo dos:
    Lo doble que aquellos.

Jane Medina

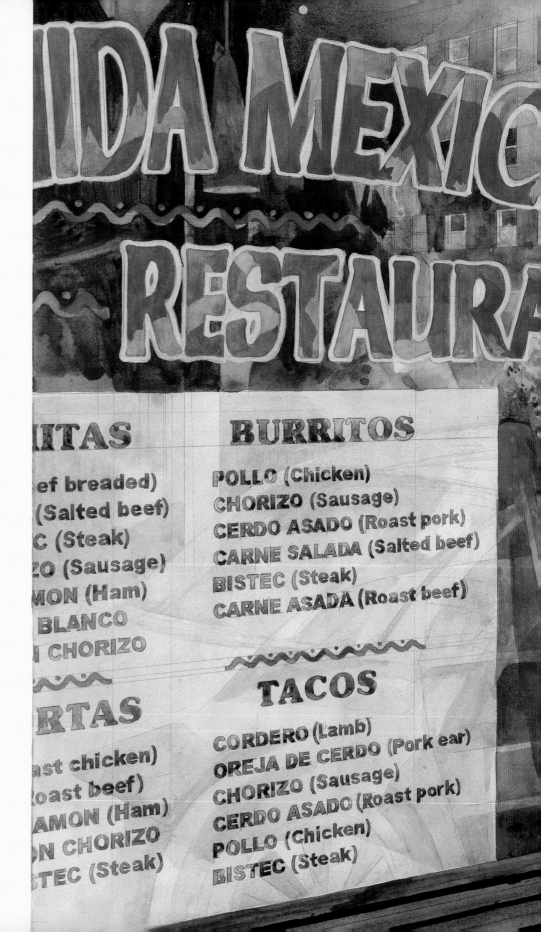

MISS STONE

My wishes gathered like ants.
I wished there was no recess.
I wished there was no first day.
I wished somebody, anybody
Would come over and ask me to play.

Then you said, "Excuse me.
Would you keep me company?
I'm feeling all alone."

Remember, Miss Stone?

I loved you that day.
You made my unhappy thoughts
Scamper away.

NIKKI GRIMES

I'M THE ONE

I'm the one
You turn your
Back on,
Never asking me
To play.

I'm the one
You heard crying,
Walking home
From school
Today.

You're the one
Who could erase
Sadness
Traced
Upon my face.

If only one day
You could see,
What fun
You'd have

Being
Friends
With
Me.

JUDE MANDELL

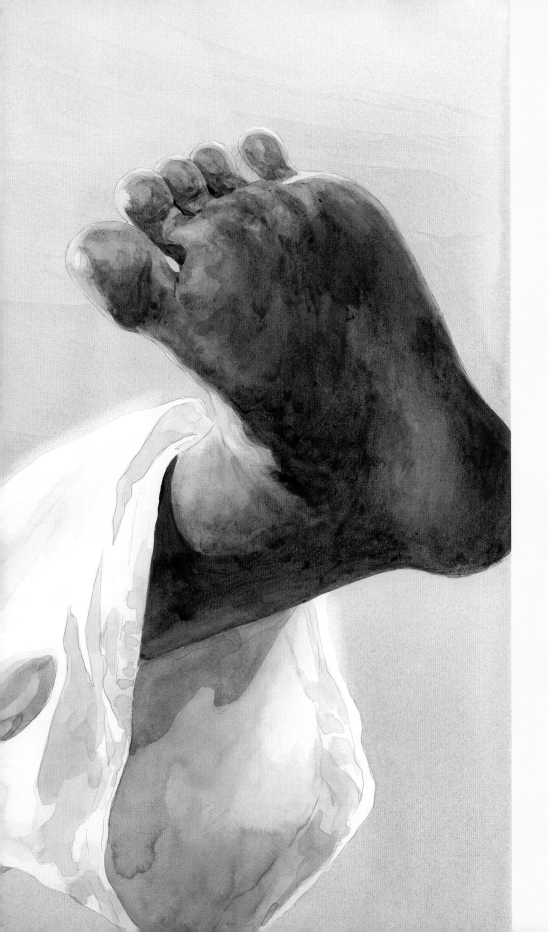

KARATE KID

I am wind,
I am wall,
I am wave,
I rise, I fall.
I am crane
In lofty flight
Training that
I need not fight.

I am tiger,
I am tree,
I am flower,
I am knee,
I am elbow,
I am hands
Taught to do
The heart's commands.

Not to bully,
Not to fight,
Dragon left
And leopard right.
Wind and wave,
Tree and flower,
Chop.
     Kick.
         Peace.
           Power.

JANE YOLEN

HERO

October comes with
Chill air—
Golden sun—

A football game—
A score of
Six to zero—

And my brother runs
A winning touchdown
And becomes
My instant hero.

TOM ROBERT SHIELDS

HIGH IN THE SKY

After supper, I sit outside
and look up at the wide, desert sky,
el cielo inmenso.

I like to count the stars.
I hear birds chirping their good-night
songs, and my family coming
to enjoy the summer breeze
drifting through the trees.

Looking high at my shimmering sky,
I count *las estrellas*
and think that far, far away

they see me and wink, wink.

PAT MORA

el cielo inmenso: the immense sky
las estrellas: the stars

LIVING ABOVE GOOD FORTUNE

I live above Good Fortune
where they catch crabs fresh

cook them any way you want
fast as you can spell c-r-u-s-t-a-c-e-a-n

I live around the corner from Heaven's Supermarket
where all lines are cash only

and you can get two for one
if you know to talk nice

I live on a street where every other thing is Lucky
and every other other thing is for tourists

My mother says,
"You don't want to go to those places"

even though she sees it in my eyes
how much I wish sometimes

but I live above Good Fortune
Lucky me

JANET S. WONG

HAMBURGER HEAVEN

He looks.	She looks.
"Hi!"	"Hi!"
"My name is Cam."	"My name is Kim."
"Been here before?"	"First time."
"Kim?"	"Cam?"
Heart beats.	Heart beats.

Love
     found
         among
   burgers,
       French fries,
and a
       mile of smiles.

LEE BENNETT HOPKINS

A YOUNG SOLDIER

A young soldier
returns home—

keeping
miles of memories
sealed
within

one
heartbreaking
boyish
grin.

PRINCE REDCLOUD

FIREFIGHTER FACE

Trickles of sweat etch silvery trails
down wind-bitten cheeks coated with ash.
Curtains of vapor, with each breath he exhales,
wreathe his tired smile, his drooping mustache.

Framed by smoke-smudged wrinkles,
soot-black eyebrows cannot hide
a flash of blue eyes that twinkle
with strength and triumphant pride.

MARY E. CRONIN

AUNT MOLLY SKY

You can read so many things in her face.
Like a cloud touched by the breath of wind
one shape, then another takes its place
as even the trees lean close and listen.

One of her eyes is half closed—distant—
seeking legends in the listening night.
The other is bright as Grandmother Moon
guiding us with a gentle, changing light.

The lines in her face are not from worries.
Like small streams running to the sea
they flow with laughter and memories
of how things were and still might be.

A certain smile always appears
when she feels a story about to come.
That smile is like an open door
All of us, young and old, are welcome.

I see her there by the fireplace.
Her cheeks are aglow as if from within.
She speaks the words that bring magic to this place.
"Here my story camps, let the tale begin."

JOSEPH BRUCHAC

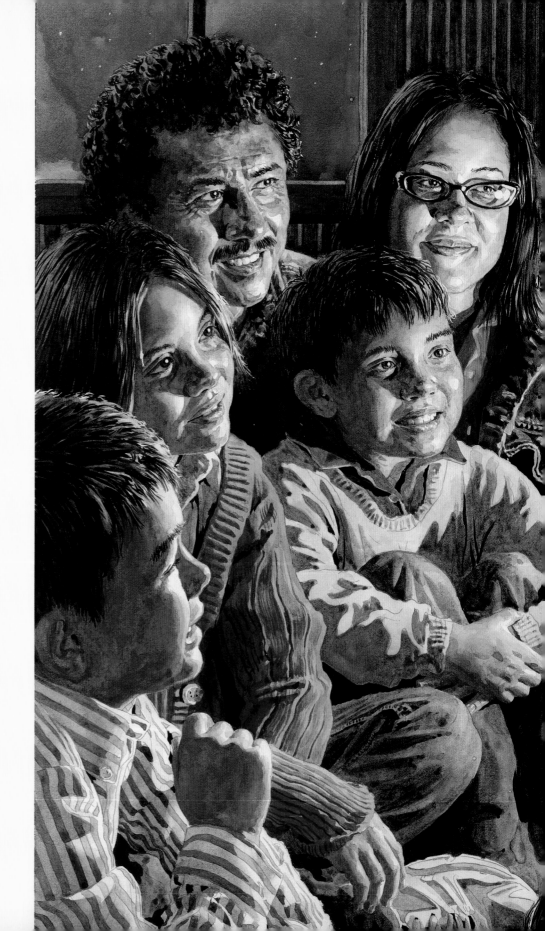

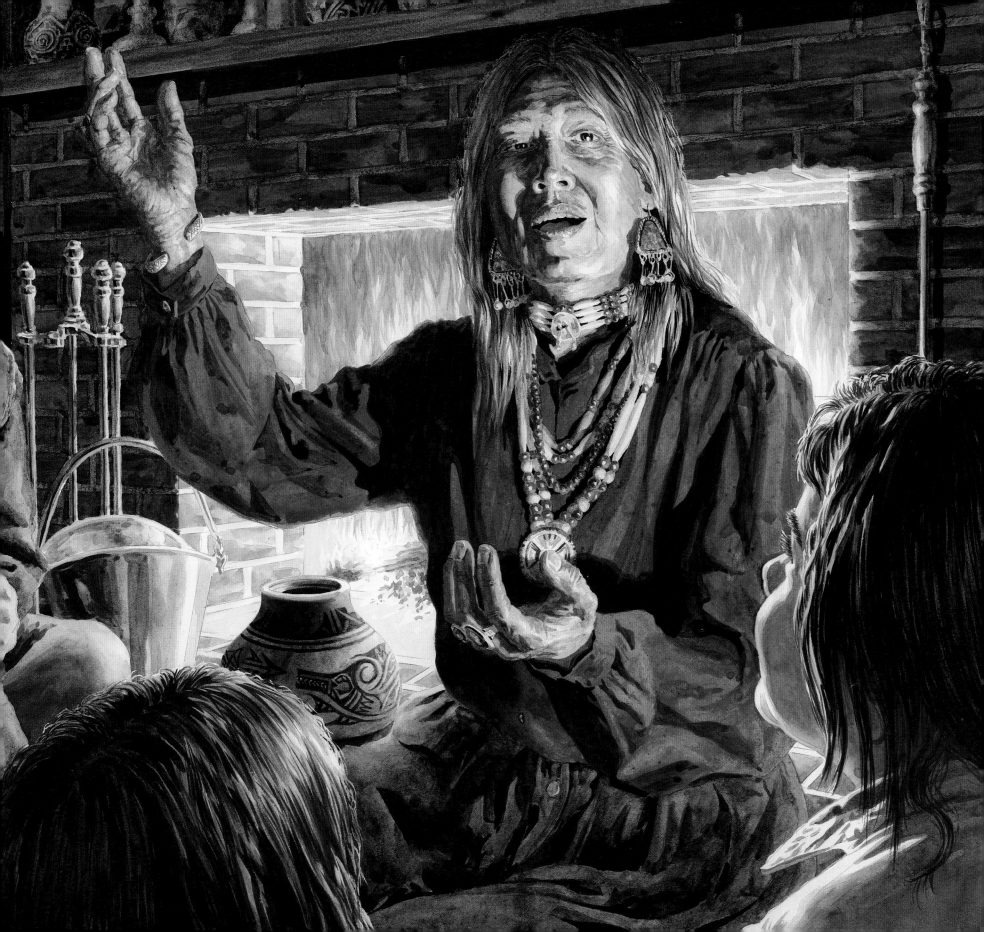

ABUELA

Her face, a lacework of courage;
Her brow, brown as settled earth;
Her chin, worn thin, a point of pride;
Her cheeks, soft antiques of the sun;
Her smile, a profile in mischief,
Latina, *abuela*, she is everyone
Of us come from otherwhere,
Happy to call another stratosphere
Home.

J. PATRICK LEWIS

abuela: grandmother

MY PEOPLE

The night is beautiful,
So the faces of my people.

The stars are beautiful,
So the eyes of my people.

Beautiful, also, is the sun.
Beautiful, also, are the souls of my people.

LANGSTON HUGHES